THE BASEBALL BOOGEYMAN

THE BASEBALL BOOGEYMAN

Written by James Gelsey

SCHOLASTIC INC.

New York   Toronto   London   Auckland   Sydney
Mexico City   New Delhi   Hong Kong   Buenos Aires

ISBN 0-439-55713-5

Copyright © 2004 by Hanna-Barbera.
SCOOBY-DOO and all related characters and elements
are trademarks of and © Hanna-Barbera.
CARTOON NETWORK and logo
are tradmarks of and © Cartoon Network
(s04)
Published by Scholastic Inc. All rights reserved.
SCHOLASTIC and associated logos are trademarks and/or
registered trademarks of Scholastic Inc.

Designed by Louise Bova

12 11 10 9 8 7 6 5 4 3 2 1   4 5 6 7 8 9/0

Special thanks to Duendes del Sur
for cover and interior illustrations.

Printed in the U.S.A.
First printing, November 2004

Chapter 1

Late one night, baseball star Luis Santiago was practicing his hitting inside an empty baseball stadium. A pitching machine fired baseballs over the plate. Luis hit each ball hard. The balls flew out of the park. Luis wanted to break Cab Craig's all-time home run record.

Suddenly, fog covered the pitcher's mound. A ghostly figure

wearing an old baseball uniform stepped out.

"I'm warning you!" shouted the ghost. "You'll be sorry if you try to break my record!"

Then the ghost pitched a series of fireballs right at Luis. As Luis tried to fend them off, the ghost

disappeared back into the fog. Luis was scared! He ran away from the field.

The next day, the Mystery Machine pulled up to the outside of the stadium.

"Wow! Cookie Company International Park!" Shaggy exclaimed. "Like, what a great name for a ball field."

"Reah, rookies!" Scooby barked.

Velma explained that the old baseball stadium sunk into the ground when its foundation gave out. The new stadium was built right on top of it.

The gang headed inside the stadium. Out on the field, Scooby saw a giant grizzly bear following one of the players. He ran over and bit the bear's tail. Surprised, the bear reached up and took off his mask. The man inside was J. T. Page, a pitcher. J. T. told the gang how he

was cut from the team. He was allowed to stay only if he became the new mascot, Mr. Grizz.

Fred asked where he could find Luis Santiago, and J. T. pointed to the side of the field. There, Luis Santiago was being interviewed by Bob Taylor, one of the team's announcers. Fred and the gang walked over.

"Excuse me, Mr. Santiago?" said Fred. "I'm Fred Jones, the winner of the 'Meet Luis Santiago' contest." Fred started talking about every single one of Luis Santiago's at-bats. He was Luis's biggest fan.

Velma and Daphne rolled their eyes. "It's going to be a long afternoon," Daphne said.

Chapter 2

At the game that night, Bob Taylor's voice echoed throughout the stadium.

"Strike three! And the Grizzlies retire the side in the second inning," he announced. As the teams switched positions on the field, Daphne felt a few raindrops. A moment later, a large metal roof slid over the top of the stadium.

"Okay, Grizz fans, Steve Powell here to call the bottom of the second," came another voice over the speakers. "And up first is Luis Santiago."

Luis stepped to the plate. The crowd cheered. The first pitch sped by Luis. It was a called strike. Luis turned to the umpire to argue the call. But when he looked up he saw the baseball ghost!

"I warned you! Now you'll be sorry!" the ghost shrieked. The ghost shot his hand up toward the roof. As he did, the lights along the roof exploded, one by one. The stadium was thrown into darkness. The fans leaped from their seats and ran out screaming.

A little later, Luis and the gang were sitting in the locker room. Luis told the kids what had happened the night before.

"Do you know who this baseball boogeyman might be?" Daphne asked.

"Of course," Luis answered. "He's

the ghost of the all-time home run leader, Cab Craig."

"G-g-g-ghost!?" Shaggy and Scooby cried. Scooby jumped into Shaggy's arms.

At that moment, a woman dressed in a business suit burst into the room. She hurried over to Luis.

"Great news, Luis! We're the

lead story not only on the Sports Station, but the evening news, too!" she exclaimed.

Luis introduced everyone to Ann Summers, his publicist. Ann really wanted to take advantage of the publicity about the ghost. But Daphne thought Luis should rest up for the next game instead. Luis agreed with Daphne. Ann was so angry she stormed out of the locker room.

"Don't worry, Luis," Fred said. "You concentrate on baseball. Leave the crime solving to us. We're going to bring that phony phantom to justice."

Chapter 3

The gang decided to start with the exploding lights. They found their way to the lighting grid high above the ball field. They discovered some safety harnesses used for changing the lights. Fred, Daphne, and Velma put on the harnesses and carefully lowered themselves down to examine the lights.

"Jinkies! Take a look at this!" Velma called.

Fred and Daphne joined Velma. She was pointing to a generator wired into the lighting system.

"This must have been used to overload the lights and make them explode," Velma said.

Meanwhile, Shaggy and Scooby

prepared a picnic on the ball field. Shaggy carefully laid out all of their snacks. Scooby started digging a hole to bury the leftovers for later. Shaggy started digging, too. Suddenly, Scooby let out a yelp. Shaggy looked down and saw that Scooby had uncovered a large metal hatch beneath the dirt. Shaggy pulled on it, and the hatch suddenly opened. Shaggy and Scooby tumbled down into the darkness.

"HELLLLLLLLLLLP!" they cried.

The two buddies landed with a THUD! Shaggy and Scooby looked around and saw they were in the middle of an old locker room.

"Like, this must be that old stadium that sunk into the ground," Shaggy said. They stood up and started exploring. "I'll bet the baseball ghost uses these tunnels to get around under the field!"

As they turned a corner, they ran smack into the ghost!

"Zoinks!" Shaggy cried. "Let's go, Scoob!"

Shaggy and Scooby ran down a long tunnel. The ghost was right behind them. They found a ladder and scrambled up. At the top, they pushed open a wooden hatch and popped up into the back of the new stadium's locker room. A closet door was right in front of them. So they hid inside.

The ghost popped his head up and looked around. He climbed up into the room and walked over to the closet door. But instead of opening it, he locked it. Then he turned a dial on the wall. The closet started filling with steam.

"Man, this isn't a closet!" Shaggy moaned. "This is a steam room. And we're locked inside!"

The ghost laughed maniacally as Shaggy and Scooby pounded on the door.

"HELLLLLLP!" they cried.

Chapter 4

Fred, Daphne, and Velma heard their friends' screams and came running. They tried to unlock the door, but it was stuck. Fred grabbed a baseball bat that was lying nearby. He knocked off the doorknob. The door fell open, and Shaggy and Scooby stumbled out. They were covered in sweat.

"Like, thanks, Fred," Shaggy gasped. "One more minute and we would've been a couple of roasted peanuts!"

"We're glad you two are all right," Daphne said. "But we've got a few more things to check out."

The gang walked back onto the

field. As they looked around, Daphne noticed that the lights were still on in the announcer's booth. The gang went upstairs to check it out. Inside the booth, one wall was covered with pictures of

Bob Taylor playing baseball. Fred noticed an old team photo that included Bob Taylor and Cab Craig. But before he could show it to the others, strange organ music filled the air.

Everyone followed Fred down the hall to the organ booth. Inside, a shadowy figure was hunched over the organ. The figure turned around with an evil laugh.

"Jinkies! It's the baseball ghost!" Velma exclaimed.

"Run!" Fred shouted.

The gang took off down the hall and disappeared around the corner. The baseball ghost raced after them. The gang ran through the stadium, trying to lose the ghost. They made their way across the field and onto the bleachers.

"No sign of that baseball baddie," Shaggy said. "I think we shook him."

Suddenly, the bleachers started to shake.

"I think I spoke too soon," Shaggy moaned.

Beneath the bleachers, the baseball ghost was loosening the bolts holding the stands together. The bleachers started to fall apart! The gang leaped to safety just as the last of the bleachers fell.

As the dust cleared, Fred dangled from the edge of the next

tier of seats with Daphne, Velma, Shaggy, and Scooby clinging to him.

"I've heard about hanging around a ball park," Shaggy said. "But this is ridiculous."

Chapter 5

One by one, the Mystery, Inc. members pulled themselves to safety. They walked back toward the main part of the stadium. Suddenly, a bright flash blinded them.

"Gotcha!" a woman yelled. It was Ann Summers. "Hey, wait a minute. You aren't the baseball ghost."

Velma asked why Ann wanted a picture of the ghost. Ann explained that while she was driving home in the storm, she realized that a photo of the ghost would be great publicity for Luis.

After Ann left, Daphne told the others that Ann was lying. "She said she was driving home when she got the idea," Daphne said. "But did you notice that her shoes were dry? That means she never left the building."

A loud grinding sound suddenly echoed through the stadium. They looked up and saw the roof slowly beginning to open.

"Someone's trying to let the rain in to ruin tomorrow's game!" Velma said.

The gang headed for the roof. But when they got to the top they discovered that the control panel was on the other side of the roof deck.

"Gather round, everyone, I have a plan," Fred said. He gave everyone a job.

"What about me?" asked a strange voice. The gang hadn't noticed that the baseball ghost was standing beside them! The ghost gave a deep, booming laugh that frightened the gang. They ran to the edge of the roof. It was sliding open slowly. Everyone but Scooby jumped across. Scooby stood at the edge, looking down and whimpering.

"Come on, Scooby!" Shaggy called. "You can do it!"

The ghost came closer to Scooby.

Scooby gathered his courage and leaped into the air. He sailed up . . . and then down, missing the other side of the roof.

"Oh, no!" Daphne cried. "Scooby didn't make it!"

Chapter 6

As soon as he saw Scooby jump, Fred leaped into action. Grabbing one of the rope harnesses, he jumped off the roof and grabbed on to Scooby. The two of them plummeted down, but the rope pulled taut a few feet from the ground.

"And we're . . . safe!" Fred called. He sounded just like an umpire.

Daphne, Velma, and Shaggy ran to the roof controls. They stopped the roof and then reversed it so it would close. The ghost was not expecting the sudden change in motion. He lost his balance and tumbled off the edge of the roof! As he fell through the air, the ghost grabbed onto Fred's rope to slow down.

Fred shook the line a few times, knocking the ghost loose. He fell toward the field. But he didn't stop—he kept on going and disappeared into the turf!

"Jeepers! He went right through the field!" Daphne exclaimed.

Velma, Daphne, and Shaggy ran down to the field to help Fred and Scooby. Then they all made their way down to the buried stadium.

In one of the rooms, Shaggy
noticed a great big barrel.

"A pickle barrel!" he said. Shaggy
opened the barrel, took one whiff,
and quickly closed it. "Man, these
things sure are ripe!"

"Reah! P.U.!" Scooby said,
holding his nose.

Fred opened the pickle barrel

again. But instead of pickles inside, Fred discovered baseballs soaking in gasoline.

"So that's where the ghost gets those flaming fastballs of his," Velma said.

Fred checked his watch. "It's getting late," he said. "I say we call it a night and pick things up tomorrow before the game."

When they arrived at the stadium the next day, the gang heard J. T. Page arguing with someone. The other person wanted Mr. Grizz to be fired out of a cannon. J. T. refused to do it and quit. As J. T. stormed off, Bob Taylor stopped in front of the gang.

"That kid should consider himself lucky," he said. He explained how tough it had been for him to find any work after he left baseball. He did whatever he could just to get by. "I painted houses, gave piano lessons, and even worked as a dog groomer." He demonstrated his grooming skills on Scooby. Then he excused himself to go up to the announcer's booth.

Just before game time, Fred and the others sat with Luis in the empty locker room. Luis said that most of the other players were scared off by the baseball boogeyman. Without enough players, they'd have to forfeit the game.

"Forfeit? No way!" Fred said. "You have to break that record!"

"And we need to wrap up this mystery," Velma said.

"And I know how we can do both!" Fred said. "Listen up, everybody."

Chapter 7

Later that night, the crowd roared as the Grizzlies took to the field.

"It's a beautiful night for baseball!" Bob Taylor announced. No one noticed that some of the players looked a little different. Fred was at third base, Velma at second, Daphne at first, and Shaggy was shortstop. Scooby stood on top of the dugout. He was dressed in the Mr. Grizz costume.

The game got under way, and the Grizzlies made it through the top of the first inning. After the first two batters struck out, Luis Santiago came up to the plate.

"Okay, fans, Steve Powell here with you to call the rest of the first inning. Now stepping up to the plate is Luis Santiago."

Luis nervously looked around. There was a puff of smoke, and the baseball ghost appeared on the pitcher's mound. He hurled a flaming fastball at Luis. But Luis managed to hit it safely off to the side.

"Now, Daphne!" Fred called.

Daphne ran to the side of the field. She opened a valve, turning on the sprinklers! The ghost's

flaming baseballs quickly went out.
But the angry ghost charged
toward Daphne!

Velma suddenly drove onto the
field in a baseball-shaped golf cart
and scooped Daphne up. They
zoomed toward the Grizzlies'
dugout.

"Phase two, Shaggy!" Fred
called.

Shaggy and Scooby raced across the field and climbed on top of the dugout. He aimed the automatic pitching machine at the ghost and fired away. Shaggy moved the dial on the machine from FAST to WAY, WAY FAST. Baseballs pummeled the ghost.

"Strike! Ball! Strike! Ball! Ball!" called Steve Powell.

The ghost leaped up on top of the dugout. Shaggy and Scooby huddled together at the edge of the dugout roof. The ghost loomed over them and lunged forward to grab the two friends. Shaggy and Scooby separated at the last second, and the ghost lost its balance. He

tumbled over the edge of the
dugout and into the cannon.

"We did it!" Shaggy cheered.
"Hold your ears, Scooby!"

Shaggy grabbed the cannon fir-
ing switch and pushed the button.
Nothing happened. He and Scooby
leaned over the edge to take a look

when KA-BOOM! The cannon went off, shooting the ghost, Shaggy, and Scooby into the air. The three of them tumbled through the air and landed in the safety net behind home plate.

"And he's out!" announced Steve Powell.

Chapter 8

The crowd was silent as they watched all of the events unfold on the stadium's jumbo screen. A close-up of the ghost filled the screen. Shaggy reached over and took off the ghost's mask.

"Bob Taylor?!" the crowd gasped.

Stadium security helped Shaggy, Scooby, and Bob Taylor climb out of the net. Then they handcuffed Bob Taylor.

Fred, Daphne, and Velma
explained how the clues all fit
together. After they learned that

Bob Taylor used to give piano lessons, they remembered that they
had found the ghost playing the

organ. And after seeing all of Bob's baseball pictures, they realized that he and the ghost were both lefties.

"But why would you do this, Bob?" asked Luis.

"Because Cab Craig was my best friend," Bob replied. "I wanted his record to stand forever!"

The umpire walked over to them. "What do you say we play some baseball today?" he asked.

A little later the game began again. As the gang watched from box seats behind the Grizzlies' dugout, Luis Santiago came up to bat. The pitcher went into his windup and delivered a blazing fastball. Luis swung and an enormous *CRACK* filled the air. The ball sailed higher and higher and cleared the scoreboard on the far side of the field.

The crowd went nuts as Luis Santiago triumphantly ran the bases.

"Luis Santiago has broken the record! He's broken the record!"

Steve Powell cheered. "All with a little help from . . ."

Scooby's face suddenly filled the giant screen.

"Scooby-Dooby-Doo!" he cheered.